UNOFFICIAL GUIDE

VICTORY ROYALE
GUIDE
FORTNITE

TIPS AND STRATEGIES TO DEFEAT YOUR ENEMIES

Michael Davis

CrackBoom! Books is an imprint of Chouette Publishing (1987) Inc.

Chouette Publishing would like to thank the Government of Canada and SODEC for their financial support.

Bibliothèque et Archives nationales du Québec and Library and Archives Canada cataloguing in publication
Title: Unofficial Guide Victory Royale Guide Fortnite: tips and strategies to defeat your enemies / text, Michael Davis; illustrations, Epic Games.
Names: Davis, Michael, 1981- author. | Epic Games, Inc., illustrator.
Description: Series statement: Fortnite
Identifiers: Canadiana 20190017678 | ISBN 9782898021336 (softcover)
Subjects: LCSH: Fortnite Battle Royale (Game)—Juvenile literature.
Classification: LCC GV1469.35.F67 D38 2019 | DDC j794.8—dc23

Legal deposit – Bibliothèque et Archives nationales du Québec, 2019.
Legal deposit – Library and Archives Canada, 2019.

CONTENTS

INTRODUCTION

Fortnite isn't just a game, it's an obsession. There's something about its combination of fast-paced combat, freewheeling game environment, and innovative building system that makes players want to play it in every free moment—all in pursuit of that elusive Victory Royale!

Of course, with so many players dedicating themselves to mastering this robust, complicated game, you'll need an edge if you want to come out on top.

This guide is that edge. In the following pages you'll learn the best building strategies and combat tips, as well as some little-known intricacies of the game. Give them your time and attention, and you'll be flossing over your downed foes in no time!

Enough chit-chat. Let's board the Battle Bus!

CHAPTER 1:
THE DROP

Don't assume that Fortnite begins after you've touched down on terra firma. If you ignore the strategic element of the drop from the Battle Bus, you're wasting an opportunity to get a leg up on your opponents. In this section you'll learn the pros and cons of specific starting locations, as well as some tips on how to make the most of your drop.

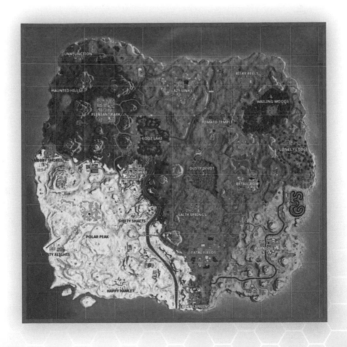

TOP DROP LOCATIONS

In the following section, we'll be discussing some specific locations that are particularly good starting points. Be warned that Fortnite is a constantly evolving game. As of Season 7, locations like Flush Factory and Greasy Grove are gone, replaced by new areas like Polar Peaks, Frosty Flights, and Happy Hamlet. Developers are always tweaking the Fortnite world, so make sure to keep up with their changes at the game's official website.

TILTED TOWERS

Tilted Towers is one of the most lucrative loot spots in Fortnite, boasting tons of treasure chests, great materials to harvest, and of course, plenty of rare weapons!

Unfortunately, everyone knows this. Tilted Towers is a hot spot for experienced players, who use their superior combat skills to take down the competition and gain a strong early-game advantage.

Even if it isn't a great starting spot for beginners or intermediate players, Tilted Towers is an excellent location to work on your combat. Maybe your chances of surviving the first few minutes are pretty slim, but you can develop your skills by dropping here again and again and picking fights until you're taken out.

Also, consider switching to spectator mode, to the POV of the person who took you out. They're probably a solid player and you can learn a lot from their approach.

> **TIP** ▶ IF A PLAYER TAKES YOU DOWN, HE'S PROBABLY BETTER THAN YOU. SWITCH TO THEIR POV TO IMPROVE YOUR KNOWLEDGE OF THE GAME.

LOOT LAKE

This location's name is no joke: Loot Lake does provide powerful items, including rare weapons, definitely making it worth a visit. Like most good loot locations, however, it's a popular drop spot.

Loot Lake is fairly central in the map, which puts you in a good position to react to the storm.

Be aware that the lake is dotted with islands that also deserve your attention: Most of them harbor worthwhile loot. The terrain of Loot Lake is a mix of high and low elevations, so if you plan to make this your regular starting point, low elevation is the way to go: It gives you a quicker land, and a slightly faster start to the game.

FROSTY FLIGHTS

This is a great new loca-
tion, added in Season 7,
that gives you access to the
most exciting new vehicle in
Fortnite, the X-4 Stormwing
(see the vehicles section for
more information on this
awesome plane).

The Stormwing is a great choice for squad games, as it can
carry five players, including the pilot, and has enough weapons
and supplies for all of them. Be aware that it's situated at the
edge of the map, if you don't manage to snag a plane, you'll be
sprinting to beat the storm. Leave yourself plenty of time.

VIKING OUTPOST

This is a very popular drop location for not only its loot chests
but also its abundant supply of harvestable metal and stone. Its
northern location positions you well for your next move into the
map. Just make sure you keep an eye out, because other players
also know the value of Viking Outpost, and they won't make your
life easy.

HAPPY HAMLET

This is a fairly large location, which means you have a decent chance of getting in and grabbing some loot without encountering another player.

If you're worried about conflict with other players, though, there are some warehouses in the northwest corner of E9 on the map. These are not well-marked, which means you'll run into

fewer enemy players and be able to loot in relative peace.

POLAR PEAK

This is a new area in Fortnite, and mostly covered in snow. However, as the season has progressed, new areas to explore have been revealed.

DROP TIPS

CHAIN LOCATIONS

Never start a game of Fortnite without first deciding where you're going to land. This allows you to get to the ground as quickly as possible, with a clear idea of which buildings and loot locations to prioritize.

When deciding on a drop point, the first choice to make is whether you want to land in a crowded, popular section of the map, or on the outskirts, where competition is less fierce, but equipment is scarce.

Plan ahead and know exactly where your second and third loot location will be. That way, you can focus on staying alive, rather than making broad strategic decisions on the fly.

DON'T DEPLOY YOUR GLIDER UNTIL THE GAME FORCES YOU TO

In these early minutes of the game, efficiency is essential. This means choosing your drop location before the game starts, as mentioned above. It also means not stopping to see the sights. Stay in free-fall as long as you can to gain a few precious seconds of early glider deployment. Since the glider deploys automatically at a certain elevation, feel free to push your free-fall as long as possible.

TERRAIN AFFECTS WHEN YOUR GLIDER DEPLOYS

The lower the elevation, the longer you stay in free-fall. Keep this in mind when you pick your landing spot. If you plan right, you can do most of your dropping over a low-elevation area (for example, water). When your glider deploys, you can still cover a fair amount of ground while you glide to your landing. Experiment to see how far your glider will get you: It's farther than you think!

PAY ATTENTION TO THE BATTLE BUS ROUTE

The Battle Bus Route gives you information about the locations of other players. Get in the habit of noting what areas the bus passes over, and how popular they are as landing spots. In this way you can build up a loose idea of where players might be concentrated on the map.

WATCH THE SKIES

While you float gently into the chaos that is Fortnite, keep an eye out for other players gliding in.

If you're familiar with the drop area in relation to the richest loot locations, you can probably guess what building another player will prioritize. If you find a great weapon early on, this may help you quickly catch up with and eliminate other players in the area, or inspire you to stay away from certain areas of a drop location where the fighting is likely to be heavy.

REMOTE VS. CROWDED

Any of the named areas will be reasonably popular with the 99 other players, so expect heavier action when landing in denser areas. Bear in mind that if you stick to remote areas, the loot will be lower in quality, so it's a trade-off. There are many YouTube tutorials identifying remote locations that offer a quiet start with a decent amount of loot.

HAVE A BATTLE PLAN AND STICK TO IT

A huge element in winning a complex game like Fortnite is reducing as much as you can to muscle memory. Overthinking is dying. An easy strategy is to figure out your general route during the game. The best players develop a favorite route every season, and stick

to it. By all means, plan an alternate route to keep things interesting, but generally speaking, don't make decisions on the fly about where to loot and explore. By then it's too late.

KNOW WHAT BUILDINGS TO PRIORITIZE

If you find yourself favoring a specific area, take some time to really explore it. Evolve a rough plan that includes two or three routes you can take through the area. It's a good idea to have some backups in case you want to avoid other players, but if you like an area, get to know it like the back of your hand.

HANG BACK ON THE BATTLE BUS FOR EASY KILLS

In most Fortnite sessions there are a few players who have to leave the game, for whatever reason, before it gets started. If you wait until the Battle Bus forces you to jump, you'll land with all of these abandoned players and score some easy kills. Of course, you're giving up a major time advantage for no serious gain in resources, so it's a heavy price to pay. But if you're feeling like you need a couple of easy fights, this is where you'll find them.

CHAPTER 2:
LOOT

Fortnite is a frantic race for survival: Every player starts with nothing, then improves their situation by finding both loot and better equipment. Smart looting pays off when your tech edge allows you to eliminate other players and plunder their hard-won equipment. It never hurts to have an assault rifle when you face off against a player with a handgun.

For this reason, looting is a huge priority in Fortnite Battle Royale. There are seven sources of loot. This does not include materials harvesting, which is discussed in a different section of this guide.

CHESTS

Chests are a great source of loot, containing a (somewhat) randomly generated mix of weapons, consumables, ammo, and building material. Chests glow in-game and make a distinct noise, so keep your ears open. If you ever hear a chest above you, don't try to get to it by breaking through the ceiling: A chest will disappear if you destroy the surface it rests on.

SUPPLY DROPS

Supply drops are a leg up from chests, as they always contain a legendary weapon. Supply drops are signaled by a loud noise, after which the drop floats down from the sky to a landing site marked by smoke. Be forewarned that everyone else is aware of the drop and will also be interested in scooping up its bounty. Or worse, that they'll set up nearby to pick off careless players mesmerized by that sweet loot.

Always tread carefully when investigating a supply drop, and be ready for a firefight. When collecting from a supply drop, take a moment to build a simple protective structure to increase your odds of surviving the looting spree.

If you decide to camp out near a supply drop and try to ambush other players, hold off on attacking until the player is in the middle of looting the supplies. They will be distracted and easier to pick off. Of course, once they're eliminated, whatever loot they've snagged is yours.

Finally, you can shoot at a falling supply drop to damage it, which will cause its location to be marked on your map. Even if you don't plan to duke it out with anyone for the contents, it's helpful to glance at the map and see where players may be gathering in above-average concentrations.

VENDING MACHINES

This loot source allows you to trade resources you've harvested for specific loot. There is a different item for each of the three resources—wood, brick, and metal.

LLAMAS

Llamas are not exactly common, but they're a great source of loot. They give you a ton of building material, ammo and consumables. Make sure to protect yourself with a 1x1 structure, because llamas take longer to open than a regular chest does, and that makes you vulnerable to attack.

 TIP TAKE COVER WHEN OPENING A LLAMA AS IT TAKES LONGER THAN A REGULAR CHEST.

FLOOR LOOT

Floor loot is exactly what it sounds like—it's just sitting out there. This is the most plentiful type of loot in the game, but don't expect much in the way of rare items. Still, it can be a great source of ammo and consumables.

AMMO BOXES

Guess what's inside these boxes? That's right: Ammo. Which you're going to need a lot of in order to win the Battle Royale, so keep an eye out for these boxes.

OTHER PLAYERS

This is one of the best ways to acquire equipment. The player you just took out was carefully building up their collection and probably has a few great items. As the game wears on, the quality of loot from a downed player will increase.

Try to figure out what you'd like to snag before you approach the downed player, since you want to spend as little time as possible in the area. Other players may have heard your battle and be waiting to pick off the weakened survivor. Always check your surroundings, and consider a quick 1x1 to protect you.

Finally, equip a pickaxe while looting in these situations. The game automatically drops one of your weapons if you pick up more consumables than you can stack in your inventory slot, but you can't drop the pickaxe, so make sure it's selected to avoid this possibility.

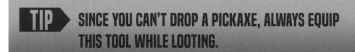

TIP SINCE YOU CAN'T DROP A PICKAXE, ALWAYS EQUIP THIS TOOL WHILE LOOTING.

CHAPTER 3:
HARVESTING/BUILDING

A fun and unique feature of Fortnite is the building system. Winning the game is nearly impossible unless you become experienced in the nuances of building structures. That's because building is not just about a cool fort for the endgame, or a temporary structure to allow yourself to heal. It's a tool that can be used offensively to push in on another player (to get closer without exposing yourself to damage) and gain the high ground. It can even be used tactically, in combination with editing, to eliminate opponents.

Of course, you can't build if you don't have materials, so this section will also look at some tips for efficiently harvesting material. You don't want to be caught without resources during a build-battle.

MATERIALS

There are three types of building materials in the game—wood, brick, and metal—each with different characteristics.

WOOD

The weakest and fastest building material is also the easiest to harvest. Wood is the go-to material for Fortnite players who have incorporated building into their offensive strategy.

STRUCTURE	INITIAL HEALTH	FINAL HEALTH	HEALTH GAIN	BUILDING TIME
Wall	90	150	18 HPS	3.5 Sec
Floor	75	140	18 HPS	4 Sec
Stairs	75	140	18 HPS	4 Sec
Roof	75	140	18 HPS	4 Sec

Best Source
Wooden pallets give at least 60 wood per stack.

Pros
In the early and mid-game, wood is essential. It builds the fastest, and is found everywhere in the environment. Another advantage of wood is that as it builds, it offers better visibility than brick or metal, so you can keep an eye on your opponent while staying protected.

Cons

Wood makes a fairly loud sound as you build, which can attract the attention of other players. As the weakest building material, it isn't very good for building permanent bases. Its low final health means it can be demolished easily.

BRICK

Brick is the middle ground between metal and wood. If you're using brick, in most cases it's probably because you wanted to build with metal, but ran out.

STRUCTURE	INITIAL HEALTH	FINAL HEALTH	HEALTH GAIN	BUILDING TIME
Wall	90	300	20 HPS	10.5 Sec
Floor	75	280	18 HPS	11.5 Sec
Stairs	75	280	18 HPS	11.5 Sec
Roof	75	280	18 HPS	11.5 Sec

Best looting sources

Big rocks, statues, walls and buildings made of brick.

Pros

Stronger than wood, and faster to build than metal.

Cons

The least useful of the building materials. While it never hurts to have some on hand, why choose brick when wood is faster and metal is stronger?

METAL

The sturdiest building material, but the slowest to build. Metal is great for creating sturdy late-game permanent structures. It's a hunker-down material.

STRUCTURE	INITIAL HEALTH	FINAL HEALTH	HEALTH GAIN	BUILDING TIME
Wall	90	500	18 HPS	22.5 Sec
Floor	75	460	16 HPS	24 Sec
Stairs	75	460	16 HPS	24 Sec
Roof	75	460	16 HPS	24 Sec

Best looting source

Cars give at least 50 metal.

Pros

Metal is harder for other players to see through than brick or wood, so if you're looking for a little privacy in your base, this is your best choice. Metal can also withstand a great deal of punishment, so consider it as a building material in the later parts of the game. Metal is quieter to build with than wood.

Cons

Metal takes the longest to build, so in a fast-paced game like Fortnite, you should avoid it in the early game, when you want to prioritize speed and versatility.

TYPES OF BUILD

There are four basic types of structure in Fortnite, each of which can be further edited into more complex shapes. Ramps and walls are definitely the most common of the build types, but the roof and platform type also have their uses.

RAMPS

Ramps are arguably the most useful build type in Fortnite. They quickly allow a player to gain that elusive high ground, and also work well with walls to create cover with variable exposure. A ramp allows you to micromanage how much of your body is exposed when you shoot from your position on the ramp. This is essential for conserving shields and health.

Ramps also help you get to the top of mountains or buildings quickly, or even to approach someone else's tower so you can take them on. Ramps collapse when their base is shot out, but if you've built next to a mountain, the ramp adjacent will count as "grounded."

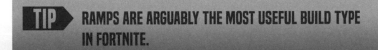

TIP ▶ RAMPS ARE ARGUABLY THE MOST USEFUL BUILD TYPE IN FORTNITE.

WALLS

Walls pair well with ramps for building basic cover such as panic ramps, and are also essential for building a protected fort. Walls are in a 3x3 square pattern, and are a great point of reference for fall damage: If you are more than three walls' worth of height off the ground, you'll start taking damage from a fall. Walls can be edited to add windows, doors, and even arches. You can also edit them from their default height to be shorter.

PLATFORMS

This building structure is generally laid on the ground, but can also be used as a roof, or a bridge connecting two structures. Platforms can also be edited, although you are mainly limited to removing one of the 2x2 squares. Note that if you remove a square from the floor, the edge of the floor adjacent to the remo-ved portion will now have a lip that pokes up. The lip doesn't offer much cover, even if you crouch. Ramps are much better cover during sustained long-range combat.

ROOFS

Roofs are handy when protecting yourself from an opponent with a height advantage. They can also be dropped over enemy structures to trap opponents inside their own build after you toss in a grenade. This build type can be useful as a type of shallow ramp when built on the ground. Or it can be placed over dropped items and equipment that you are unable to collect, to hide them from other players.

EDITING STRUCTURES

While it's a priority to become familiar with quick builds, eventually you will want to practice edits to existing structures. While you probably won't use a lot of these edits, they allow a great degree of customization. You'll definitely want to become familiar with editing windows and doors into walls, though, as these have a tactical advantage we'll discuss later.

STRUCTURES OBEY PHYSICS (SORT OF)

There's nothing quite like seeing an insanely high tower poking up into the sky, or a physically impossible ramp that goes on for miles. These unlikely structures give the impression that Fortnite is a world without gravity or physics. But the structures in Fortnite obey natural laws in an important and deadly way— without a foundation, any structure will crash to the ground.

Always be aware that as you go higher, someone can knock out the bottom of your build. It can be as simple as a single shot from a rocket launcher. Falling from a height equivalent to three walls will start to cause damage, and you can die without special equipment like balloons to slow your fall from eight walls.

TURTLING

Turtling is a simple strategy when you need to regain health safely by popping health or shield items, setting up a campfire, or simply taking a moment to breathe.

> **TIP** TURTLING IS A DEFENSIVE STRATEGY THAT ALLOWS YOU
> TO REGAIN HEALTH UNDER A PROTECTIVE BUILD.

Four walls and a roof will give you a bit of protection, with a fairly low cost of resources for relative safety. However, keep in mind that these small structures are a sure sign to experienced players that you are turtling, and may encourage them to push in for a kill. Always scan the area for enemy players before turtling, and certainly never turtle in the middle of a battle. If you are near established in-game structures, consider just running into a building to regain your health.

USEFUL BUILD PATTERNS

Over time, players have discovered certain structures work better than others. Here are a few types of structure that should be part of any player's build strategy.

PANIC RAMP

This is a wall with a ramp leading up to it. The ramp is great for positioning—it protects all but the smallest vulnerable area of

your player—and the wall stops people from easily destroying the ramp. Even if the wall is destroyed, the ramp is still sound, and you can put it between you and your attacker while you build more walls.

Feel free to build walls around the side and back for more protection, and you can build a second ramp facing the other direction (imagine the ramps form a V). This will allow you to cover your flank from attackers as well.

If you build walls around your panic ramp, consider adding a door. You'll want a quick exit strategy if someone starts lobbing grenades or drops down from high ground.

COVERED ESCAPE

Sometimes a sniper sets up well above you, perhaps on a mountain. You're caught in the open. How do you escape? Create a wall and a roof to protect yourself (turtling), then edit a door in the wall. As you run for cover, continue building platforms

connected to the top edge of the walls of your temporary fort (the platform acts as a roof above you to block an attack from above). Make sure you add the odd wall as you go so the whole roof doesn't collapse and destroy the original structure.

DOUBLE RAMP

When you're pushing closer to an enemy, a ramp is a great way to gain a height advantage while also protecting yourself from attack down below. Your opponent can, however, shoot out the bottom of the ramp, bringing you down and possibly causing fall damage. To lessen the chances of this happening, many players will zigzag as they build, creating a ramp that is two pieces wide. This way multiple pieces must be destroyed to bring the whole ramp down.

REINFORCED RAMP

Rather than just building a ramp as you push up on an opponent, consider spending a little more material to build a floor and a wall first. This creates a more stable structure that is harder and takes longer to shoot out. Building this structure fast takes practice, but the cost of materials is well worth the extra safety.

BASE

A more permanent base is a common strategy in the late stages of a Fortnite match, since you won't have to abandon it to the storm. Build such bases out of sturdier materials like brick and wood, and be careful about building too high. Your base may be strong, but by this point in the game, multiple players will probably have enough RPG ammo to blow up your foundation and cause fall damage.

BUILDING AND HARVESTING TIPS

PRACTICE BUILDING IN CREATIVE MODE

Fortnite now has a creative mode, where you can play without the constant fear of someone shooting you. Explore this mode and practice building some of the above structures. In this way you can start to understand which hotkeys are most useful to customize so that you can build without thinking, like the pros.

HIT THE BLUE TARGET WHILE HARVESTING

As you swing your pickaxe at a harvestable resource, take note of the circular blue icon that appears. If you strike at this instead of at a random spot, you will harvest more efficiently.

MOVING VS. STATIONARY HARVESTING

If you walk right next to the item you wish to harvest, the blue target will stay still, making harvesting quicker. This goes directly against one of the major pieces of advice in this guide, which is to NEVER stay still. But sometimes you're in a situation where you're confident no one is around, and standing still to harvest a larger object will get the job done faster. Rules are made to be broken, after all.

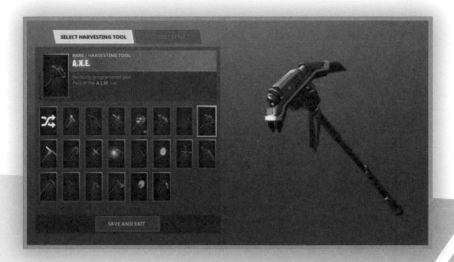

That said, in areas of high player concentration, get into the habit of constantly moving while harvesting. It might take a little longer, but who knows how many snipers may be out there waiting for you to slow down?

DON'T HARVEST THE WHOLE TREE

As you run along the terrain harvesting trees, you leave behind an easy-to-follow trail of stumps that gives away your location. You also create a sound cue of falling trees that's hard for nearby players to miss. Consider harvesting only part of the tree, or even better, creating false trails of downed trees to lure an unsuspecting player into a trap.

DON'T GET CAUGHT LOW ON MATERIALS

Building is an essential component of winning Fortnite Battle Royale, so get used to thinking of materials as essential. Try to never be caught with less than 250 of materials, and try to enter the endgame with at least 600 (of 999) of each material to make sure you can build a quality fort to defend.

CHAPTER 4:
WEAPONS

In Fortnite, every player has a limited inventory of five slots for equipment, including weapons. Those slots also do not include your pickaxe or any collected building materials.

A limited inventory is a fun aspect of the game because it forces you to decide which items you value over others. Let's begin with the relative values of the weapons in Battle Royale.

There are many weapons in Fortnite, and in the early game you need to take advantage of whatever you find.

WEAPON CLASSES

Not all weapons are created equal. Fortnite Battle Royale is designed to reward players for staying active and searching out rare and competitive loot opportunities. As a result, the longer you stay in the game, the more powerful the weapons in play are. Memorize their class colors so you'll know when you've found a valuable one. The following colors are ordered from most common to rarest, with a corresponding bump in stats that will make purple and orange your new favorite colors.

COMMON   UNCOMMON   RARE   EPIC   LEGENDARY

WEAPON TYPES

Each weapon has a slightly different feel, even compared to weapons of its own type. Over time you will discover your preferences, but you won't always have access to your favorites, so it's a good idea to become proficient with as many weapons as you can.

HANDHELD GUNS

Handguns are most useful at mid to close range. As such, they can't compete for valuable inventory slots with the immensely more important shotgun, assault rifle, sniper rifle, and explosives weapons. In the early game, however, they can give you a valuable advantage.

The different handgun types offer substantially different features, so always be aware of your load-out and prioritize your handgun based on your current equipment's blind spot.

Pistols

Pistols are found in only three colors: gray, green, and blue. They hold up to 12 rounds, and their relative accuracy makes them most effective over short and medium distances. In a pinch, they can even be effective during an ambush.

ICON / RARITY	DPS	DAMAGE	MAG.SIZE
COMMON	155.2	23	16
UNCOMMON	162	24	16
RARE	168.7	25	16

Suppressed Pistol

Quieter and more powerful than a regular pistol, this weapon can be useful for take-downs that won't attract attention.

ICON / RARITY	DPS	DAMAGE	MAG.SIZE
RARE	175.5	26	16
EPIC	189	28	16

Revolver

The revolver has less ammunition than the pistol but does more damage. Like the pistol, it's available only in gray, green, and blue.

ICON / RARITY	DPS	DAMAGE	MAG.SIZE
COMMON	48.6	54	6
UNCOMMON	51.3	57	6
RARE	54	60	6

Hand Cannon

Based on the Desert Eagle handgun, this is the strongest pistol in the game. A solid headshot will deal 75 points of damage, but at the expense of decreased accuracy. This weapon, which comes in purple and orange versions, is also harder to find.

ICON / RARITY	DPS	DAMAGE	MAG.SIZE
EPIC	60	75	7
LEGENDARY	62.4	78	7

Scoped Revolver

This weapon does decent damage, especially if you use its scope to line up a headshot. Decreased magazine size and loss of peripheral awareness while aiming are its major drawbacks.

ICON / RARITY	DPS	DAMAGE	MAG.SIZE
EPIC	67.2	42	6
LEGENDARY	70.4	44	6

SHOTGUNS

Nothing is more effective than a shotgun when it's time to get up close and personal, the way you do fairly often while scrambling for loot in your early game. Closer is better in shotgun combat, and the weapon's relatively slow reload rate means you have to make shots count. On the other hand, the shotgun's pellet spread means you don't have to be as precise to inflict damage from close up. Spend some gaming sessions dropping into highly populated areas to practice shotgun combat. A single shot to the head is often enough to down opponents... if you can hit the target.

But forget about using shotguns for mid to long-range combat. Almost any other weapon is more effective at wearing down your opponent's shields. Save the shotgun for the close-up coup de grace.

There are several types of shotgun:

Tactical Shotgun

As far as shotguns go, the tactical has a decent rate of fire, and can be found in gray, green, and blue classes.

ICON / RARITY	DPS	DAMAGE	MAG.SIZE
COMMON	100.5	67	8
UNCOMMON	105	70	8
RARE	111	74	8

Pump-Action Shotgun

This type trades off rate of fire for increased damage. A single headshot will kill a player with full health, though an opponent with a full health and shield will not go down as easily.

ICON / RARITY	DPS	DAMAGE	MAG.SIZE
UNCOMMON	66.5	95	5
RARE	70	100	5
EPIC	73.5	105	5
LEGENDARY	77	110	5

Heavy Shotgun

This shotgun trades off the heavier damage of a pump action for greater range. (If you're using a shotgun, though, range shouldn't be your primary concern.) The weapon also holds seven rounds at a time, which means less reloading than other shotguns. But keep this in mind: If you can't take down an opponent in a couple of shots, then you need to practice more with the shotgun.

ICON / RARITY	DPS	DAMAGE	MAG.SIZE
EPIC	73.5	73.5	7
LEGENDARY	77	77	7

Double-Barrel Shotgun

Shotguns are all about short-range combat, and this one excels at it. Dealing 120 damage even without a head shot, this weapon is extremely effective. It's the shotgun you want in your inventory. Just make sure you practice close-range combat so you can use it effectively.

ICON / RARITY	DPS	DAMAGE	MAG.SIZE
EPIC	216.6	114	2
LEGENDARY	228	120	2

SUBMACHINE GUN (SMG)

With a very fast firing rate and high damage per second, these are great alternatives to the shotgun for close-quarters combat. Unlike the assault rifle class, though, the submachine gun suffers substantial performance loss at medium range.

Use a submachine gun like an assault rifle, shooting in controlled bursts to conserve ammo. These weapons can devour your ammo supply before you know it. The different types of submachine gun include:

Submachine Gun

Essentially a poor man's assault rifle, the submachine gun has a more limited range and does less damage than its bigger automatic cousin in the game.

ICON / RARITY	DPS	DAMAGE	MAG.SIZE
COMMON	204	19	30
UNCOMMON	216	20	30
RARE	228	21	30

Compact SMG

The Compact SMG deals about the same amount of damage, but can hold more rounds per clip. Also, the DPS is greatly reduced.

ICON / RARITY	DPS	DAMAGE	MAG.SIZE
EPIC	210	20	40
LEGENDARY	220	21	40

Suppressed SMG

This weapon trades off damage for stealth, so if you're not trying to keep a low profile, the other SMGs are better tactical choices.

ICON / RARITY	DPS	DAMAGE	MAG.SIZE
COMMON	180	22	30
UNCOMMON	189	23	30
RARE	198	24	30

MINIGUN

At first glance, this weapon might seem more at home in the assault rifle category, but it actually uses light ammunition.

The minigun has limited value in your mid to endgame load out, but it can be very effective in destroying enemy structures. This weapon has no reload, so you can fire as long as you want until you run out of ammo. Be aware that it has a brief warm-up period, so there will be a slight delay when you pull the trigger before it starts firing.

Miniguns are also good at keeping heat on an enemy player—not giving them room to breathe. If you're up against an opponent who throws up structures as cover, the minigun can quickly overwhelm them, leaving no time to strategize or fight back. However, its accuracy is not great, so over time you would be advised to replace this fun but limited weapon with something better.

ICON / RARITY	DPS	DAMAGE	MAG.SIZE
EPIC	216	18	–
LEGENDARY	228	19	–

ASSAULT RIFLES

No weapon load-out is complete wit-hout rifles. In fact, it's recommended that you spend two valuable slots on rifles, one for assault rifles, and the other for snipers. Assault rifles are  arguably the most important basic weapon in Fortnite, and are generally considered the most versatile weapon in the game due to their dynamic range and ease of use.

Assault rifles have a high damage output, and can quickly deplete enemy players' shields. Remember to fire in short bursts to improve accuracy and conserve ammo. Unlike those of sniper rifles, assault-rifle rounds hit their target instantly after leaving your gun, so there's no need to correct for gravity, as there is with sniper rifles. You want to keep your cross-hairs squarely on your opponent.

Basic Assault Rifle

This is the most common assault rifle. The lower-level versions of this weapon are generally referred to as M16s, while the epic and legendary tier, known as SCARs, are widely considered to be some of the best weapons in the game.

ICON / RARITY	DPS	DAMAGE	MAG.SIZE
COMMON	165	30	30
UNCOMMON	170	31	30
RARE	181.5	33	30
EPIC	192.5	35	30
LEGENDARY	198	36	30

Burst Rifle

Firing wild bursts of ammunition that are very inaccurate, the burst rifle is only effective at short distances. Available in all classes, it's a weapon you shouldn't hesitate to lose once a better one comes along.

ICON / RARITY	DPS	DAMAGE	MAG.SIZE
COMMON	109.7	27	30
UNCOMMON	117.9	29	30
RARE	121.9	30	30
EPIC	130.1	32	30
LEGENDARY	134.1	33	30

Scoped Assault Rifle

This rifle uses a scope similar to a sniper rifle's and has very good accuracy when zoomed. It can be very useful in the end-game, when players are forced to build forts close to each other. But rather than rely on this weapon, consider spending time with a sniper rifle, which is more finicky, but also more effective.

ICON / RARITY	DPS	DAMAGE	MAG.SIZE
UNCOMMON	80.5	23	20
RARE	84	24	20

Thermal-Scoped Assault Rifle

Similar to the scoped rifle, but with the added benefit of providing a thermal view of the battlefield that reveals enemy players hiding behind forts and other kinds of cover.

ICON / RARITY	DPS	DAMAGE	MAG.SIZE
EPIC	64.8	36	15
LEGENDARY	66.6	37	15

Suppressed Assault Rifle

An assault rifle that trades off other benefits for quieter shooting.

ICON / RARITY	DPS	DAMAGE	MAG.SIZE
EPIC	176	32	30
LEGENDARY	181.5	33	30

Heavy Assault Rifle

This rifle trades off magazine size for increased damage, as the name would suggest.

ICON / RARITY	DPS	DAMAGE	MAG.SIZE
RARE	165	44	25
EPIC	172.5	46	25
LEGENDARY	180	48	25

SNIPER RIFLES

New players hate the sniper rifle. It takes a long time to reload, and it's tough to aim accurately. Finding one in the first place can be hard. Besides which, these are the only weapons in the game affected by physics, which means that you have to take gravity into account when you're aiming at a distant target. Finally, they zoom in on your enemy, which limits your awareness of the immediate area while you're lining up a shot, making you vulnerable to someone sneaking up on you.

So why bother with a sniper rifle? How about their incredible power over long distances? No other weapon in Fortnite can take out a player from so far away. And of course, if you're halfway across the map, you're less likely to take damage. Long-term survival is what Battle Royale is all about. This is the weapon that separates the noobs from the winners. Ignore it at your peril.

Suppressed Sniper Rifle

A decent sniper rifle, but like all suppressed weapons, its stats suffer a bit for the added benefit of a quieter shot.

ICON / RARITY	DPS	DAMAGE	MAG.SIZE
EPIC	33	100	1
LEGENDARY	34.7	105	1

Bolt-Action Sniper Rifle

A good choice for a sniper rifle because of its rarity (only top-tier versions exist). Scoop this one up if you find it.

ICON / RARITY	DPS	DAMAGE	MAG.SIZE
RARE	34.7	105	1
EPIC	36.3	110	1
LEGENDARY	38.3	116	1

Hunting Rifle

The hunting rifle is an interesting variation on the sniper-rifle class because it lacks tactical optics (i.e., no extreme zoom-in option). At first glance, this may seem like a huge disadvantage, but this rifle is popular with pro players with a lot

of experience because it doesn't reduce your view of the playing field. It's a good choice for confident players who know they can make the shot and don't want to lose valuable visual information. The more you build up your skill with the sniper rifle, the more you'll come to prefer it.

ICON / RARITY	DPS	DAMAGE	MAG.SIZE
UNCOMMON	68.8	86	1
RARE	72	90	1

Heavy Sniper Rifle

This beast trades off firing rate for a massive amount of damage, taking players down 150 points with a single shot. A player favorite for destroying structures late game, it can deal more than 1,000 damage to buildings. Note that the falling speed is lower than that of other sniper rifles, so you don't have to correct for distance as much.

ICON / RARITY	DPS	DAMAGE	MAG.SIZE
EPIC	49.5	150	1
LEGENDARY	51.8	157	1

LAUNCHED EXPLOSIVES

One of your inventory slots should be dedicated to explosive weapons. These are good not only for dealing massive damage to enemy players, but also for attacking enemy bases in late-game combat.

Explosive weapons cause splash damage, which means they don't demand the same precision as a sniper rifle or similar long-range weapon. The trade-off is a relatively slow firing rate, so line up your shot well, and keep moving afterward, because you might not get another chance!

These weapons take time to reach their target, so while they're effective at long range, they give an enemy plenty of time to take cover. They're most effective against enemy structures, which can't get out of the way.

Grenade Launcher

Now we're talking! The grenade launcher is a great tool for demolishing enemy forts, and gives you more room to breathe than lobbing grenades. This weapon is relatively rare, occurring only in blue, purple, and orange classes. When you find one, don't hesitate to upgrade from simple thrown grenades.

ICON / RARITY	DPS	DAMAGE	MAG.SIZE
RARE	100	100	6
EPIC	105	105	6
LEGENDARY	110	110	6

Rocket Launcher

It's a pleasure to watch Twitch players wreaking havoc in the endgame with an RPG stocked with well-hoarded ammo. This is the rarest and most powerful weapon in the game. It's incredible at destroying forts and bases, and it has both a high rate of fire and a large blast range. It can even be used effectively at close range with structures in play. This weapon is amazing. If you see it, snag it.

ICON / RARITY	DPS	DAMAGE	MAG.SIZE
RARE	82.5	110	1
EPIC	87	116	1
LEGENDARY	90.75	121	1

THROWABLE EXPLOSIVES

Like handguns, throwables have strengths and weaknesses that suit them for particular situations. Some cause splash damage, others drain health, and still others, like the boom box, have the fun but deadly effect of forcing your enemy to dance helplessly for five seconds. Know each weapon's capabilities so you can use it effectively.

Throwable weapons are a one-time use item, so don't be careless with them. Unlike bullets, they have an arcing trajectory which can take some to get used to. Practice so that in a tense situation you're confident your throwable will land where you want it to.

Throwables can be very useful when dealing with teams of players, as their splash effect can affect multiple players at once.

Grenades

Take them where you can find them early game, but don't hesitate to replace them later on with the much more useful grenade launcher or RPG. Grenades can serve you well, though— dealing 100 damage which can splash onto nearby players. While they can instantly wipe out an entire shield or health bar with this kind of damage, they can also be clumsy to use, with their arced throwing pattern. If you hold down your trigger button you'll see a curved line that projects where your grenade will go.

Grenades are mainly useful in early-game encounters when you're in close quarters while looting buildings, and can lob one into an enclosed space when an opponent isn't paying attention.

Impulse Grenade

This type of grenade doesn't cause damage, but instead acts as a portable jump pad, shooting nearby players into the air (including you, if you're too close). While these grenades can certainly be used to catch an opponent off guard,

Impulse Grenades are most useful for generating quick movement—for example, to escape the storm or propel injured teammates out of a bad situation so you can tend to them safely.

Stink Bomb

Yet another type of grenade that deals 5 damage every 0.5 seconds. The stink bomb lasts for 9 seconds, dealing its damage to any enemies within range. In all honesty, this weapon is not ideal in Fortnite, but it can be useful to force occupants of enclosed spaces or secure forts to evacuate without destroying them.

Dynamite

This explosive causes 70 damage and explodes 5 seconds after a throw. Dynamite's main advantage over regular grenades is that it can inflict more damage to enemy structures.

Boogie Bomb

The Boogie Bomb is fun, no doubt about it. Forcing your opponent to dance is awesome! This bomb does 0 damage; essentially, we're dealing with a stun grenade here. It can be useful in team games, where an efficient player can take out several opponents while they dance helplessly, unable to attack. In any case, the shotgun is excellent for finishing off a player who's busy boogying.

Boom Box

This is another weapon that is effective at taking down structures. It lasts for a whopping 20 seconds or until destroyed by depleting its 400 HP. It deals periodic blasts of 200 damage to structures (not players) in the immediate area, and is susceptible to gravity, meaning that it will fall if the structure it's resting on is destroyed.

BEST WEAPONS
IN FORTNITE

The following are considered to be some of the best weapons in the game, so if you see them, make room in your inventory! Keep in mind this list is based on solo play. Some weapons perform better in a team setting, where players take on complementary roles and no one person has to do everything.

This list is organized according to a weapon's performance in two categories:

POWER

In an intense game like Fortnite, every shot counts. The best weapons deliver a powerful punch, meaning a quicker battle, less damage for you, and increased chances of long-term survival.

RANGE

Sniper rifles are best suited to distant engagement with the enemy, and shotguns to encounters at close range. But the best weapons have versatility in their effective ranges.

MUST-HAVES

The following weapons are relatively easy to operate, and provide versatility in solo play. They offer great damage and are found in both low and medium rarities. If you see these, scoop them up!

1. Pump Shotgun
2. Suppressed Assault Rifle
3. Heavy Shotgun
4. Rocket Launcher
5. Compact SMG

PRETTY AWESOME

These weapons are not as effective as the Must-Haves, but are definitely valuable. When utilized by a competent player, they can be very effective.

– Heavy Assault Rifle

– Tactical Shotgun

– Hand Cannon

– SMG

– Grenade Launcher

– Burst Assault Rifle

– Heavy Sniper Rifle

– Suppressed Sniper Rifle

– Scoped Revolver

GRAB 'EM IF THERE'S NOTHING BETTER

We're rapidly sliding down the scale in terms of usefulness. Still, a decent weapon, even a common one, is better than none.

– Bolt Action Sniper Rifle

– Assault Rifle

– Hunting Rifle

– Minigun

– Thermal Scope Assault Rifle

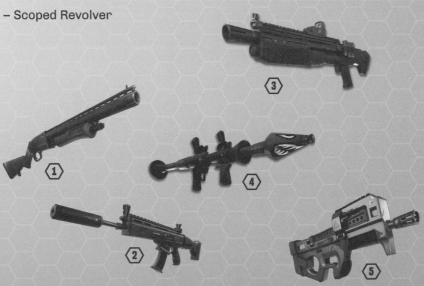

WEAPON TIPS

SNIPER RIFLE: TAKE THE SHOT

Assuming you're not hurting for ammo or worried about keeping a low profile, it can be a good idea to try taking difficult shots with your sniper rifle. You might get lucky, and practicing your quick draw is always a good idea.

Most new players avoid the sniper rifle because its finicky aiming system intimidates them. Spend some time with the weapon, and experiment with taking shots you normally wouldn't. It's the only way to develop an intuitive feel for this long gun.

SNIPER RIFLE: MOVE AROUND BETWEEN SHOTS

Always move around after one or two sniper rifle shots, as another sniper may be lining you up for an attack. Don't let them get a bead on you. Keep them guessing.

SNIPER RIFLE: THE ONLY WEAPON WITH A DROP-OFF

The sniper rifle is the only weapon whose bullet is affected by gravity. For all other weapons, just aim it where you want it! For sniping, the farther away you are, the more you'll want to raise your aim. You'll rarely need to use more than the second tick on the aiming scope, so practice in order to get a good sense of when to go to first tick or second.

DON'T FORGO EXPLOSIVES

Some players avoid explosive weapons because of the danger of splash-back damage. Don't be one of them. A good stock of grenades is an essential part of more advanced strategies. If grenades scare you, spend a dozen games experimenting with them. There's a reason they're in the game, and, if you avoid them, you're cutting off some awesome strategy approaches.

GET TO KNOW YOUR WEAPON CAPACITY

In single-player shooters, we've all developed the habit of reloading before our clip is exhausted. Because nothing is worse than needing to reload in the heat of the battle. But in a competitive game like Fortnite, you need to modify this strategy. You don't have the luxury of reloading whenever you want. ANYTHING that makes you vulnerable, even for half a second, is to be avoided whenever possible. This means reloading only when necessary, and only when you're in a safe spot. Don't be the player who has plenty in the clip but reloads anyway—then gets taken out.

BULLETS LEAVE TRACERS

Bullets leave a trail in Fortnite. If someone you can't see is taking potshots at you, watch for this telltale clue about their position.

KEEP A COOL HEAD

This is more of a philosophical tip, but don't let it mess you up if you miss a few shots in a row. It happens to the best of us, and getting tense about it will only make things worse.

If you get frustrated, consider a quick retreat using a launch pad or a rift, and take a few deep breaths. The extra oxygen in your lungs will focus your mind and help with nerves. Speaking of taking care of your real body...

TAKE A BREAK

Don't forget to take a break every half hour to get up and walk around. You'd be surprised how much a little physical exercise will help you in-game.

CHAPTER 5:
ITEMS

There are quite a few items that you can loot in the game. Some items provide healing, other can be used for offensive purposes. From deadly traps to restorative campfires, all these items help you stay in the game.

HEALING ITEMS

Even the most skilled Battle Royale players take damage from time to time. Here are some ways you can restore your health and shields to full.

MEDKIT

This restores your health to full, but takes a whopping ten seconds to activate. You can carry 3 at a time.

BANDAGES

Bandages restore 15 HP per use, but won't heal past 75 HP. You can stack this item to hold up to 15. It takes 4 seconds to take effect, so make sure you're in a safe spot.

APPLE

Found on the ground near trees, this item will replenish 5 HP. Hey, better than nothing!

SHIELD POTION

This item heals only shields, and activates after five seconds—a lifetime in Fortnite. Good thing it restores 50 shield points up to a maximum of 100. You can only carry two shield potions at a time.

SMALL SHIELD POTION

This is exactly the same as the regular Shield Potion, but only restores 25 shield points (to a maximum of 50). It only takes 2 seconds to down one of these and you can hold ten of them in your inventory. Considering the scarcity of inventory slots, these are more valuable to you than bandages.

MUSHROOM

Similar to the apple, except they restore 5 shield points instead of health. If you can find a bunch of them in one spot, the benefits can really add up!

SLURP JUICE

Instead of regenerating your stats instantaneously after its activation lag, Slurp Juice gradually restores 75 points at a rate of 2 per second—first to health, then, once health is full, to shield. You can carry two in your inventory. These healing items are quite valuable items and a top priority to collect.

CHUG JUG

This legendary item is very useful. It completely restores your health and shields, although the long activation time of 15 seconds may mean you may not live to see it take effect. You can only hold one of these in your inventory.

UTILITY ITEMS

Utility items range from extremely useful to super silly, but learning their different strengths and weaknesses will help you survive.

DAMAGE TRAPS

Spike traps that can be placed on floors, walls or ceilings. Deals 75 damage to enemy players in range.

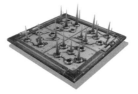

ICE TRAPS

Makes everyone's feet icy (including whoever set the trap), causing players to slip around clumsily for 15 seconds. These can be used to your own advantage (for instance, to slide downhill faster than sprinting), and can also be placed on ramps to stop enemies from using your structures to chase you. You can hold three at a time.

LAUNCH PAD

A trap that can be activated by any player, including whoever placed it. Launches players into the air so that the glider is deployed. A great item for quickly gaining the high ground!

MOUNTED TURRET

A stationary turret that can be used to attack other players. Like a minigun, the turret shoots rapidly but inaccurately. Watch out for overheating, because prolonged use can cause a forced cooldown. This is a great weapon in team play, enabling your teammates to watch your flank as you focus on dishing out mayhem.

CAMPFIRE

This item is useful for team games, as it gradually restores the health of all nearby players. You can multiply its healing effect by creating four campfires in a 2x2 square, then standing in the middle. Each campfire lasts for 25 seconds and heals a total of 50 points.

BALLOONS

The more balloons you activate, the lighter your player will be. After five balloons are deployed, you start to float; you can deploy up to six at a time. Any number below five keeps you returning to earth, but increases your loft time, like you're jumping on the moon.

You can hold up to 20 at a time, and they last indefinitely unless you float above a certain height, at which point they will explode. They will also explode (like real balloons) if another player shoots them. You can deploy your weapons while you're using balloons.

BUSH

Creates a camouflaging bush around your character which progressively falls away as you take damage. Widely considered to be a fairly basic tactic and avoided by most experienced players.

SNEAKY SNOWMAN

This item is generally considered to be more fun than useful. Disguises the player as a snowman, and also allows you to build other identical snowmen. Ten can be carried in your inventory. The decoys will disappear if enough damage is taken.

RIFT-TO-GO

This rare item creates a rift in reality that lasts for ten seconds. During that time you can enter the rift and be teleported high above your location. Even if you don't have the glider item, your glider will deploy and you can cover a lot of ground. This is a great item for escaping the storm, but you can only hold one at a time.

GLIDER

This handy item allows you to deploy a glider on command when you reach a minimum height. This airship can be very useful for building a tall structure, then gliding to your destination (it's much faster than running, and less conspicuous than a vehicle).

It can also save you from a deadly fall, and can be used offensively to descend from high ground onto an opponent's base. You can deploy your glider 10 times before running out of charges, and gliding from airtime caused by launch pads and rifts does not deplete a glider charge.

CHAPTER 6:
VEHICLES

Vehicles are an interesting addition to Fortnite, giving a strong advantage to players who go out of their way to find them.

ALL-TERRAIN KART

This vehicle is a step up from the shopping cart, which has been vaulted in recent seasons. It looks like a cross between a dune buggy and a go-kart, and can move quicker than sprinting, which makes it useful for beating the storm. With room for passengers, it can also move squad members in a team match.

ATKs are very loud and not stealthy. While the driver of the ATK is fairly well protected, his passengers are easy prey for a sniper, so a good strategy for them is to implement dances while cruising along. This keeps your character moving erratically, which makes it harder for snipers to draw a bead on them. Don't keep repeating the same dance, though: Switch it up so opponents can't anticipate it.

ATK roofs feature a jump pad, which can be handy for a quick escape or as a launch point for an attack on an enemy tower.

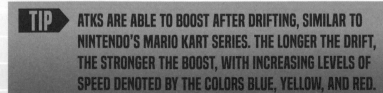

TIP ATKS ARE ABLE TO BOOST AFTER DRIFTING, SIMILAR TO NINTENDO'S MARIO KART SERIES. THE LONGER THE DRIFT, THE STRONGER THE BOOST, WITH INCREASING LEVELS OF SPEED DENOTED BY THE COLORS BLUE, YELLOW, AND RED.

QUADCRASHER

This two-person vehicle is great for ramming buildings, obstacles, or even enemy players! Think of the Quadcrasher as the game's version of a mini tank.

The Quadcrasher accumulates boost by having someone in the driver's seat. The boost can be very useful for outrunning the storm, smashing into buildings, and driving up ramps to launch massive jumps!

Note also that when the Quadcrasher rams a player it sends them flying, with a nice potential for fall damage.

X-4 STORM WING

Probably the most useful vehicle in the game, the Storm Wing is a maneuverable plane that allows players to soar above the competition. With a speed approximately four times that of sprinting, it's the fastest vehicle in the game.

The Storm Wing is also equipped with machine guns! They're best used to attack buildings or players you catch out in the open, but don't bank on many kills with them, because they're not very accurate. Also, be aware that the machine guns can overheat if you have a heavy trigger finger.

Pressing the roll button will help with sharp turns. Press both buttons and you'll fly upside down, you hot dog!

The Storm Wing holds up to four passengers and a pilot. This makes it a great transport tool, especially since its machine guns can be used to strafe enemy towers and positions from the air, putting potential snipers on the defensive. Just remember that if a Storm Wing is shot down, all of its passengers will suffer 25 damage.

Another great use of the Storm Wing is mid-air bailouts, in which you revert to drop mode, gliding down onto an unsuspecting enemy who thinks you're still on the plane!

It's not surprising that such an awesome vehicle would be rare, and as of Season 7 of Fortnite, the best place to find one is in a remote location called Frosty Flights.

CHAPTER 7:
MOVEMENT AND COMBAT STRATEGIES

Movement and combat are the most important elements of Fortnite. Nobody has ever won a Battle Royale by practicing pacifism. Faced with an ever-shrinking field of opponents, even the most conflict-avoidant player must eventually engage in movement and combat. Here are some strategies that will put you ahead of the competition.

TYPES OF MOVEMENT

There are a few specialized moves that are available to you in Fortnite. Mastering them will give you many advantages, from increased aiming accuracy to quicker moving and dodging.

WALKING

The default movement option. Walking can be useful for sneaking up on enemy players, since it makes much less noise than sprinting. It's also easier to control, so it's useful for finer movements. You can walk and crouch at the same time.

RUNNING

You probably won't do much running in this game. Sprinting is faster, and walking is more precise. Running is quieter than sprinting, however, so it can be useful for staying undetected when you are in a hurry.

SPRINTING

For most of the game, you'll probably be sprinting—if you value staying alive. While sprinting is loud and even kicks up some dust, speed is essential to staying alive in Battle Royale. Sprinting should be your default.

CROUCHING

This is an essential skill in Fortnite. In addition to making you a smaller target, crouching increases your accuracy. All of the weapons in Fortnite have a certain amount of "bloom", or bullet spread. While the exact amount depends on the quality of the weapon and your distance from the enemy, crouching automatically decreases bloom across the board. Though crouch-walking is much quieter than sprinting, it does make some noise, so don't expect to be able to sneak up on an enemy player.

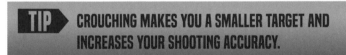

TIP ▶ CROUCHING MAKES YOU A SMALLER TARGET AND INCREASES YOUR SHOOTING ACCURACY.

GLIDING

Everyone starts off the game by gliding to the ground from the Battle Bus, but you can bring about a fresh glide by using launch pads, rifts, and the Glider Redeploy item, which was re-added to the game in Season 7. This item can be stacked up to ten deep in your inventory. Gliding is a great way to cover a lot of ground on the map, which is very handy for outrunning the storm. Just be careful not to follow a predictable path, as sharp-eyed snipers may want to bring your flight to an end.

MOVEMENT AND COMBAT STRATEGIES

NEVER STOP MOVING

Fortnite is one of the most competitive online games out there, which means that its first rule is never stand still. This applies to larger movement, too: You should always monitor where the storm is pushing you and stay constantly ahead of it.

Reloading, harvesting, building: These are all activities during which you might be tempted to stop, but you can accomplish them just as easily with constant movement.

TIP ▶ NEVER STAND STILL!

MOVE UNPREDICTABLY

Never sprint in a straight line. Always zigzag, so your movement is less predictable. And even then, don't repeat the same pattern. Similarly, throw jumping into the mix as you sprint. It doesn't slow you down in any problematic way, and it makes you a much more challenging target for snipers.

CROUCH!

This is basic stuff, but you'd be amazed how many players don't bother to crouch. Don't be one of them! Get into the habit of crouching every time you engage in long-range combat, and watch how many close calls you survive against players who are less disciplined. Crouching increases accuracy and makes you a smaller target.

BE AWARE OF YOUR ENVIRONMENT

Yes, sounds will give you clues about where your enemies are, but there's no substitute for visual information. Wherever and whenever you travel, get into the habit of jumping and quickly peeking around you. It will save your life.

JUMP SHOT

This is a difficult strategy to master, but it's totally worth it. Close-quarter combat often comes down to a single shotgun blast. While it's important to make sure your shot lands, it's just as important to make sure your opponent's doesn't. Jumping while firing shrinks your chances of taking a headshot and generally makes it difficult for your enemy to get in a good hit.

Unfortunately, jumping while shooting accurately isn't easy, so spend a few matches landing in high-density areas and wading into one-on-one fights to develop your jump-shot game. This skill alone will significantly boost your chances of winning a Battle Royale.

TIP ▶ JUMP SHOT IS A SKILL TO MASTER: BETTER CHANCE OF MAKING A HEADSHOT AND HITTING A HARD-TO-GET TARGET.

WHAT ABOUT HEALTH ITEMS?

The game renders you helpless while using bandages or potions, which is a pain, but at least it's a pain every player shares. Never pop a health item without first taking cover. In areas with buildings, this can mean hiding out indoors, or if you're out in the open, building a quick 1x1 wooden structure around yourself (don't forget a roof) so you can heal in peace.

AUTORUN

Autorun is a very handy feature. It basically automates your character's running in a particular direction; you don't have to press any buttons to keep moving. This can be extremely useful when you want to manage inventory, tweak your build settings, or simply study the map for a second. Why stand still when you can get organized and be a moving target at the same time? Just remember, autorun progresses in a fairly straight line, so don't leave it on too long. A savvy sniper will make you regret it.

KEEP THE HIGH GROUND

If you're going to implement one tip in this book, this should be it. The high ground in Fortnite is that important. It not only gives you better angles for shots and more cover, it's also psychologically effective. From the high ground, you're harder to hit and you have an extensive view point. Refer to the build section where we discuss how you can build ramps and structures to make sure you're never stuck on the ground looking up at your opponent.

USE CAMERA TO PEEK AROUND CORNERS

Fortnite's camera hangs back a bit from your player, making it different from a standard first-person shooter like *Call of Duty*. While this lets you enjoy the many dances you've learned, it also has a tactical advantage. Practice repositioning the camera when you want to see what's around a corner or obstacle without exposing yourself to attack. You should be able to sneak a peek without blowing your cover.

PATIENCE IS A VIRTUE

If you find yourself in a superior position over your opponent, it's natural to want to finish them off. Resist the urge. As the player in the weaker position they will either run away or press an attack, each one of which puts you in an even better tactical position.

WINDOWS: YOUR BEST FRIEND/WORST ENEMY

Fortnite is a very advanced video game. Windows work like windows in real life. Keep this in mind when you're entering a location with buildings. You can assess houses from afar by using a sniper scope to look for movement through the building's windows. Similarly, when you're indoors, stay away from windows. A sniper could be watching.

BUILD A RAMP BEFORE TAKING A SHOT

You've got the drop on an opponent; they have no idea you're there. It's SO tempting to take the shot before you lose your advantage. But remember, Fortnite is a marathon, and you must guard your shields and health at all cost. Always build a quick ramp before taking a shot to guarantee that if your ambush goes wrong, your opponent won't get off a lucky shot. In the final moments of the game, a lost shield could mean the difference between victory and defeat.

DON'T TAKE COVER, MAKE COVER

Fortnite isn't like regular pvp games. In Fortnite, you build. Your instinct when travelling might be to stick close to trees and rocks for cover, but that's a mistake. These obstacles will merely interfere with your builds. If someone's shooting at you your first instinct should be to throw up a ramp or wall. You have all the cover you need if you're able to build quickly.

DAMAGE COLORS GIVE YOU MORE INFORMATION THAN YOU THINK

When you land a shot on an enemy player, the game will rapidly flash the hit-point damage you've dished out. Most people don't realize that the color of the numbers is an indicator. If the numbers are blue, the player still has shields left. Yellow or white means their shields are depleted. Using this valuable information, you can decide whether to rush a weakened opponent, or wait to see whether they've popped a shield potion to become more powerful than you realized.

CHAPTER 8:
WORKING AS A TEAM

Squad games have a whole different flavor than solo play. A good team sticks together, shares resources, and follows a game plan. Here are some tips for working in a squad.

SHARE AND SHARE ALIKE

Yes, solo game in Fortnite Battle Royale is a brutal, mad dash to rise to the top. And that's part of the fun! But when you're on a team, remember that sharing weapons, ammo, items, and resources, is an essential part of the strategy.

400 wood does you no good if your teammate has none. That sniper bullet that took you down could have been avoided if your teammate was able to build. Similarly, you may be tempted to hang on to your hard-won ammo and health items, but if you don't share them with a downed teammate, they can't watch your back. Even worse, you may make yourself vulnerable if you have to revive them.

During team play get used to thinking like real soldiers. Helping one team member helps everyone. You have to stick together, even if it means giving up valuable equipment.

DON'T WANDER TOO FAR

While it's foolish for a team to stay attached at the hip, make sure you don't stray too far. Sure, when you hit a new location it makes sense for the team to fan out and each gather as many resources as they can. Just make sure you don't get carried away.

At any given time you should be 10-15 seconds maximum by foot away from your teammates. Anything more than that and you'll be too late to rescue them from a hairy situation. And vice versa.

COMMUNICATION IS KEY

Once upon a time, games didn't have instantaneous audio communication between players. Make use of it. Being able to talk to your teammates is about more than sharing a victory cheer when things are going good. You should be constantly offering up tactical information.

If you spot an enemy or some loot you don't have room for, or if you have a suggestion for the next push location, that's all valuable info. Yes, nobody likes a motor-mouth, so don't blab away about how your day went. But don't hesitate to share information, even if you think it's obvious. You may save a teammate.

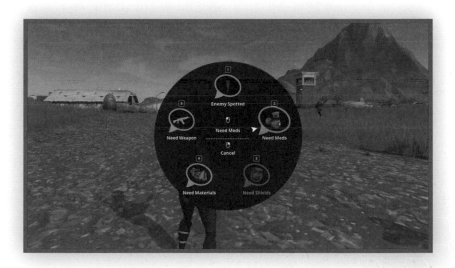

MERCY-KILL A TEAMMATE

Reviving a teammate restores 30 health. If they are below that number and you have a little breathing room, instead of handing them off a healing kit, kill them and revive. That's 30 health that didn't come out of your bandage supply. While you're at it, tell them to get their head in the game!

 REVIVING A TEAMMATE RESTORES 30 HEALTH.

RESCUING A DOWNED TEAMMATE FROM THE STORM

Things get intense when the storm comes, and you may not have time to revive a downed teammate. There's still hope! You can drop an impulse grenade to propel them out of the storm, or even build a ramp with a jump pad that they can crawl into and use to cover a lot of ground quickly. Or you can leave them to their fate.

SOMETIMES YOU CAN'T SAVE THEM

A team win is a team win. Yes, it's great for everyone to cross the finish line, but don't put your team's overall victory in danger to try and save a teammate. It sucks to leave someone behind, but you can be sure that they'd rather sacrifice themselves and be part of a winning team than lose the Battle Royale for everyone because of a mistake.

IF A PLAYER IS CRAWLING, THEY STILL HAVE TEAMMATES

The revive feature is a good way to rescue a teammate and keep them in the game, but be aware that once a player's teammates have all died, they no longer enter the crawling mode. They just die. This means you can check their team off your list!

HOLD OFF ON EXECUTING A CRAWLER

If a player is wounded and crawling, odds are that they have a teammate nearby that would like nothing more than to revive them. Rather than spending ammo up front, consider letting them crawl for a bit while you get to a safe position and try to pick off the rescuer. A couple of well-placed sniper shots could mean you get two players for the price of one.

 TIP HIDE STRATEGICALLY TO WATCH A CRAWLING PLAYER. HIS TEAMMATES ARE SURELY CLOSE BY AND CAN BE EASILY ELIMINATED.

CHAPTER 9:
ADVANCED STRATEGIES

Practicing these tips will elevate you from a good player to a great one. These advanced strategies are second nature to the pros, so make sure to spend some time perfecting them.

PLAY TO GET BETTER BEFORE PLAYING TO WIN

Hey, everybody loves coming out on top. But Fortnite's millions of fans are dedicated to improving their skills, so you'd be a fool not to work on yours, even at the expense of a win. Just like a guitar player who practices chords, then scales, then strumming patterns, be methodical. Don't just play Fortnite for a few hours and hope to win. Focus on specific skills and weapons, and make yourself a well-rounded player.

Here are some aspects of Fortnite you can focus on without worrying about being the last player standing.

- Engage in combat with different weapons and ranges
- Discover different looting locations and points of interest
- Master build techniques
- Experiment with binding keys to build quicker
- Watch from the perspective of the player who eliminated you to absorb their play style and tricks

TIP ▷ CREATIVE MODE IS GREAT TO REFINE BUILDING TECHNIQUES.

OBSERVE PLAYERS

Keep watching the game after you die. See how the other players approach the game. Reflect on what you could do differently in your next round. And what mistakes did *they* make? How can you avoid those?

CONSIDER A DEFAULT SKIN TO THROW OTHER PLAYERS OFF THEIR GUARD

Yes, it's super fun to show off your experience and personal style with the thousands of options Fortnite provides. But playing with default skins could give you an extra advantage: Other players will assume you're an easy kill.

Tricking someone into thinking you're a noob doesn't mean they won't still be dangerous, but they may let their guard down. Then you can surprise them with some advanced strategies!

RIDE THE BUS TO THE END OF THE LINE

Strategically this is an awful idea, but if you wait until the last possible moment you will be forcibly ejected from the Battle Bus, and land with all the players who were interrupted and had to abandon the match. A handful of easy kills for you, though the lost time is a high price to pay.

CONSISTENTLY ORGANIZE INVENTORY SLOTS

So much of Fortnite is minimizing thinking. It should be just you and your muscle memory, with only your critical, strategic mind working on outfoxing your opponent.

Here's a popular and effective strategy for organizing your five slots.

1. Assault Rifle
2. Shotgun
3. Sniper Rifle
4. Explosive/Trap
5. Health Item

You don't *have* to organize them in this way, obviously, but find what works for you and stick with it. When things get intense, you want to be able to access the equipment you need at the touch of a button.

THE STORM CAN BE YOUR FRIEND

Sure, the storm is a constant threat, but you can use it to your advantage.

GET CLOSE TO THE STORM

If you get ahead of the storm and camp out, you can ambush players who are too preoccupied with escaping it to notice you lying in wait.

USE THE STORM AS SAFE BORDER

Building a base with its back to the storm gives you much less area to worry about (though clever players may use our Slurp Juice tip to get behind you, so stay frosty).

USE IT TO AMBUSH PLAYERS

Using a Slurp Juice allows you to enter the storm temporarily without any major health penalties. You'll be able to ambush players who are assuming no one will attack from there.

POP A SLURP JUICE INSIDE THE STORM

Slurp Juice gradually replenishes your health, so if the storm has stopped and you want to pop in to loot a chest or grab some items, use a Slurp Juice. Even if you already have max health, you can use the Slurp Juice to move around in the storm without a health penalty!

The storm is a great place for snagging loot in relative safety, or getting behind a player base whose back is to the storm. They'll never expect you to come from inside the storm!

FALLS AND THE STORM AFFECT HEALTH DIRECTLY

Shields absorb damage from weapons and must be brought to zero before your health is affected, but be aware that falls from a height of higher than three walls and hanging out in the storm will bypass shields and directly affect your health.

THE PSYCHOLOGY OF DOORS

Open doors can tip off other players that you're inside a house, so most people shut them after they enter. While this is a great basic strategy, consider using doors in strategic ways. You might choose to leave a door open deliberately to attract a careless player, who assumes you're a noob and doesn't realize you've laid a trap. Similarly, if you don't intend to enter a house, consider opening the door as you run by. Other players may assume the place is already looted and miss out on valuable items that they could use against you later.

PICKING YOUR BATTLES

While the name of the game in Fortnite is to eliminate all the other players, there are a few situations where you might want to think twice about fighting.

THE PLAYER IS ALREADY ENGAGED IN BATTLE WITH ANOTHER PLAYER

Stay out of it until one player is victorious, then swoop in to attack the winner in their weakened state. If the two players are engaged in a frantic build battle to attain the high ground, a well-placed rocket launcher shot can destabilize their hastily constructed ramps and send both players plummeting to their deaths.

THE PLAYER SEEMS MORE EXPERIENCED

A player will betray their experience by the speed and ease with which they build structures. If you take a shot with your sniper rifle and the player's immediate reaction is to throw up panic ramps, you are probably in for a tough fight. Also pay attention to avatars, as the rarity of their skin will often give away their skill level. There's nothing cowardly about avoiding a battle with a seasoned player. Besides, the longer such a player lasts in the game, the likelier it is that they'll run into trouble on their own.

THE STORM IS TOO CLOSE

Sometimes you don't have the time for combat because you're racing the storm. Even if this frantic rush is a great time to catch opponents unaware, you just can't afford to get bogged down.

YOU'RE LOW ON SHIELD OR HEALTH

It can be tempting to battle when your shield or health are low. Who knows what juicy items and weapons your opponent will drop? But if you're in bad shape, you might want to keep a low profile and get in some looting. If you've made it to the mid-game, odds are that most of your seasoned opponents will have their health and shield maxed out.

YOUR POSITION PUTS YOU AT A DISADVANTAGE

Don't pick a fight from a distance (unless you're an amazing sniper) or if you have the low ground. If you want to last until the end, you've got to stack the odds in your favor before taking a shot.

BUILDING STRUCTURES AROUND AN OPPONENT

We often think of building as a way to protect ourselves, but if you're quick enough you can use it to trap someone. Since the enemy can't edit your builds, they'll have to use weapons to break out, while you're watching and waiting. Sometimes you can destroy a wall of another player's structure and quickly replace it with one you've built. While the player thinks they're safe, you can edit in a window and lob a grenade at them.

DON'T IMMEDIATELY LOOT A FALLEN PLAYER

We talked earlier about staying out of a battle until you can swoop in for the kill against a weakened victor. But don't let someone use this this strategy against you! Take a moment to scope out the situation to make sure you're safe before looting.

In fact, if you're in good shape equipment-wise and know that players are in the area, you can leave the loot as bait for a player who can't resist an opportunity to scavenge your spoils. From your hiding place, you can open fire.

EQUIP YOUR PICKAXE WHILE LOOTING CORPSES

You can't drop the pickaxe, so this strategy protects you from the possible annoyance of dropping a gun of value, which means you're on your way quicker—and constant movement is what this game is all about.

NO LOOT LEFT BEHIND

Sometimes your inventory is full and you're forced to leave behind some choice loot. You can expend a small amount of resources to build a 1x1 structure around the loot, making it look like a previous player turtled up in the structure for some quick healing, then abandoned it. Other players will likely pass by the hidden loot.

SOUND

If you're not playing Fortnite with headphones or a solid sound system, shame on you! Sound in the game is directional, as it is in real life. Listening tells you where things are. While you're at it, turn off the in-game music; it's just a distraction. There'll be plenty of time to rock out after the victory!

There are tons of sound cues that will help you spot, identify and track down enemy players. Here are just a few:

TRAPS

Be aware that spike traps don't make noise. For this reason, they are one of the most popular (and effective) traps in Fortnite.

GUNSHOTS

Different guns make different sounds. Listening carefully can clue you in as to whether you're hearing a close-or long-range fight, and what the various players' load-outs may be. A player firing off rockets like they're nothing probably has built up some other great loot!

BUILDS

Consider using materials of the same type if you're close to a building player that isn't aware of your presence. If they're building a fort with metal and you want to get above them, consider pushing up using metal ramps instead of the more common wood. If you can exploit the element of surprise, you'll have a significant advantage.

FOOTSTEPS

Any movement makes a sound in Fortnite, and faster movements make louder sounds. Sprinting not only creates noise, it also kicks up some dust. Keep this in mind when you are moving around. Sometimes slower is better until you have the lay of the land.

PICKAXE

The pickaxe makes a distinct sound when harvesting, which can give away your position out in the open. Keep in mind that in the early game, it's wise to harvest materials indoors, to cut down on the attention you draw to yourself.

TREASURE CHESTS AND SAFES

These make a specific sound when you're nearby. As you rush to clean out a house, take a second to search for false floors or walls that may be concealing a solid loot opportunity.

VEHICLES

Vehicles make a LOT of noise in Fortnite. Which makes sense. Players can be more vulnerable when traveling in a vehicle, so anytime you hear one is a good opportunity to get off some sniper shots. Conversely, if you are in a vehicle, know that the trade-off of your quicker movement is that every player within earshot knows what you're up to.

AMBIENT SOUNDS

If other players are blasting music while they play, it's possible their microphones will pick it up and transmit it into the game. Make sure they regret this error.

ADVANCED STRATEGIES BASED ON GAME STAGE

EARLY-GAME

Pro players know that decisions (and straight-up luck) in the early game can make or break a win. While there is a temptation to put too much focus on looting and resource gathering, a solid early-game strategy involves staying active, picking your battles, and planning in advance so that you can focus on survival rather than on-the-spot decisions. Here are some things to keep in mind.

KEY WEAPONS

You shouldn't feel comfortable with your weapon load-out until you have at least one shotgun, one assault rifle, and one sniper rifle. These three weapons cover all the bases—close-range, mid-range, and long-range combat—and will serve you well in any conflict. Yes, rocket launchers come in handy, and who doesn't like a good trap? But as you collect weapons, keep your eyes peeled for rare versions of the big three.

COLLECT PLENTY OF MATERIALS EARLY GAME

Once the map shrinks, you'll be on top of every other player and fighting for your life. Running out of materials is almost worse than running out of ammo, so make sure—during the early stages, when everyone is spread out—that you're constantly looking for opportunities to snag some resources.

DO NOT ENGAGE IN PICKAXE FIGHTS

So much of Fortnite is thinking about the long game. Your first instinct may be to pickaxe-fight if you land in the same area as another player. But even if you win, your health will be severely depleted. You'll be easy pickings for another player who didn't engage in a costly early battle.

It's much better to run inside a building and search for a weapon before taking on the enemy. While they chase you, swinging away, you may get to a weapon that allows you to take them out before they can even get a hit in.

 AS SOON AS YOU LAND, RUN FOR THE GUN.

CONSIDER STARTING FROM A HOUSE GROUND FLOOR

You've heard it before: High ground is king in Fortnite. For this reason, most players aim to land on the tops of buildings and work their way to ground level, harvesting materials and looting chests inside along the way. If it seems like you and another player are both going to land in the same general area, consider landing on the ground and working your way up to the roof. This gives you an opportunity to surprise them and get an easy kill as they come down.

HARVEST OBJECTS IN HOUSES

Early-game harvesting is key, so as you frantically loot your first chests, make sure to pickaxe plenty of furniture. In these early minutes of the match, you're vulnerable, and snagging some building materials as you gather weapons and items should be an essential part of your strategy.

IT'S ALL GOOD

A big part of Fortnite is efficiently assessing loot and deciding between what you need and what will hog valuable inventory slots and slow you down. Early game, don't worry about this. Gather everything you can. Once your slots are full, you can discard unwanted items in a random spot on the map, where other players building up their supplies won't find them and use them against you.

MID-GAME

This is from the first storm up until the very late stages of the match, when there are approximately 20-25 players left in the game. Usually the safe circle is between second and third cycle. Discussions will include the art of balancing aggressive exploration with the gathering of weapons and resources (a must for an endgame win), as well as tactics for playing defensively and picking battles.

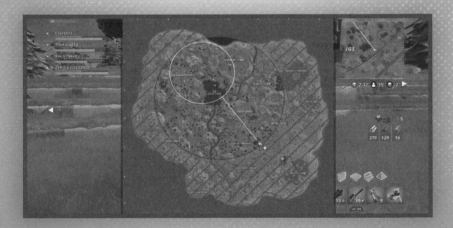

ROTATIONS

Keep an eye on what the storm is doing and plan how best to "rotate" so that you find a balance between simply running to safety and stopping along the way for some precious loot.

CAMP OR STAY MOBILE?

After the first contraction of the storm, it can be strategic to hug the edge of the storm as you look for other players. Keeping the storm to one side will greatly reduce the danger you're in as it essentially blocks off 180 degrees of attack.

Once the storm starts contracting again, however, it moves faster than you can sprint. With that in mind, it can also be strategic to head deeper into the safe zone, set up a sweet fort, and pick people off as they come running. How you choose to play is up to you, and may be affected by how aggressive the other players are. If you see a lot of players hugging the edge of the storm, maybe it's time to get a fort going for the next contraction.

DON'T GET CAUGHT OUTRUNNING THE STORM

The storm is an excellent environmental hazard that keeps Fortnite interesting by gradually shrinking the playing field. Make sure you're always aware of the incoming storm. A good mid-game strategy is to look out for players that have planned poorly and are now completely focused on trying to outrun the storm. Make sure you're picking them off, rather than being picked off.

YOU CAN SPEND A GOOD AMOUNT OF TIME IN THE STORM

It's natural to want to avoid getting caught in the storm at all costs. But remember, there's no reason to panic if you do get swept up in it; you've got a fair amount of time before your health depletes. Also, the storm area is largely depopulated, so it's a slightly safer place to loot.

BEWARE OF CLOSED DOORS IN WELL-TRAVELLED AREAS

If you find yourself mid-game in an area that has been picked over pretty well, beware closed doors on buildings (which often signal that no one has bothered looting here). Closed doors may be a trap deliberately laid by a player who came through earlier. Early game, a closed door is a great sign; mid game, not so much.

KEEP HARVESTING

Even if you've harvested a lot of resources in the early game, keep it up; don't get complacent, even though it becomes more risky to harvest. Be smart about your harvesting (for instance, avoid taking down trees all the way, as the stump and sound will give away your position). But definitely harvest. You should aim to enter the endgame with 600 materials to ensure you have the resources both to build a base and to out-build competitors.

THE STORM GETS SLOWER

The storm's speed changes each time it closes in. The first storm arrives faster than a sprint; mid game, it's slower. From the third circle onwards, you can outrun the storm. Just remember: the slower the storm, the more damage it does.

QUICK WAYS TO BEAT THE STORM

Rifts

A rift instantly transports you into the sky, just as if you were dropping from the Battle Bus. Gliding to safety, you can cover a lot of ground. Most rifts are one-time use, but there are a couple of static rift locations. These spots change season to season; stay up-to-date by searching online.

Vehicles

Vehicles can get you away from the storm quicker than sprinting, but the extra noise they create will attract the attention of enemy players.

Launch Pads

When a player comes in contact with a launch pad, they're propelled into the air high enough to deploy their glider. This is a great way of gaining the high ground and of surprising foes who have taken up positions there. Once deployed, anyone can use a launch pad, and it can be destroyed with weapons.

ENDGAME

Play strategy changes dramatically in the endgame, where there is less space to work with, resources are limited, and enemy players are using their primo equipment to take you out. Here are some tips for making yourself the last player standing.

BE PATIENT

The pace slows down a great deal in the endgame, especially compared to the frantic looting and harvesting of the early and mid-game. At this point, every shot counts, and that minor damage you took because you weren't careful could mean the difference between a win and a loss.

FORTS

Building a fort is a natural instinct in the final circle, because you know it won't get eaten by the storm. Just remember that no fort is invincible, and a really awesome fort might attract negative attention, if other players focus on you as the game's major threat. Always place your fort with one side to the storm edge. Even if players can dip into the storm to get behind you, you're reducing by one the number of sides you have to defend.

FORTIFY WITH TURRETS

Now is a good time to break out a turret to help defend your more permanent fort. Remember to protect the turret from the sides with brick or (ideally) metal walls. A turret can deter an enemy from attacking, and might even make them decide to picking a fight somewhere else during an endgame.